Jack
and the
Beanstalk

tiger tales

To Grandmama – thank you for all the books
(and for the wonderful paper they were always wrapped in!) – M. A.
For Joe & Flynn, watch out for those giants! – M. C.

tiger tales

5 River Road, Suite 128, Wilton, CT 06897
Published in the United States 2015 by Tiger Tales
Originally published in Great Britain 2014 by Little Tiger Press
Text copyright © 2014 Little Tiger Press
Illustrations copyright © 2014 Mark Chambers
ISBN-13: 978-1-58925-178-6 • ISBN-10: 1-58925-178-4
Printed in China • LTP/1400/1055/0914 • All rights reserved
10 9 8 7 6 5 4 3 2 1
For more insight and activities, visit us at
www.tigertalesbooks.com

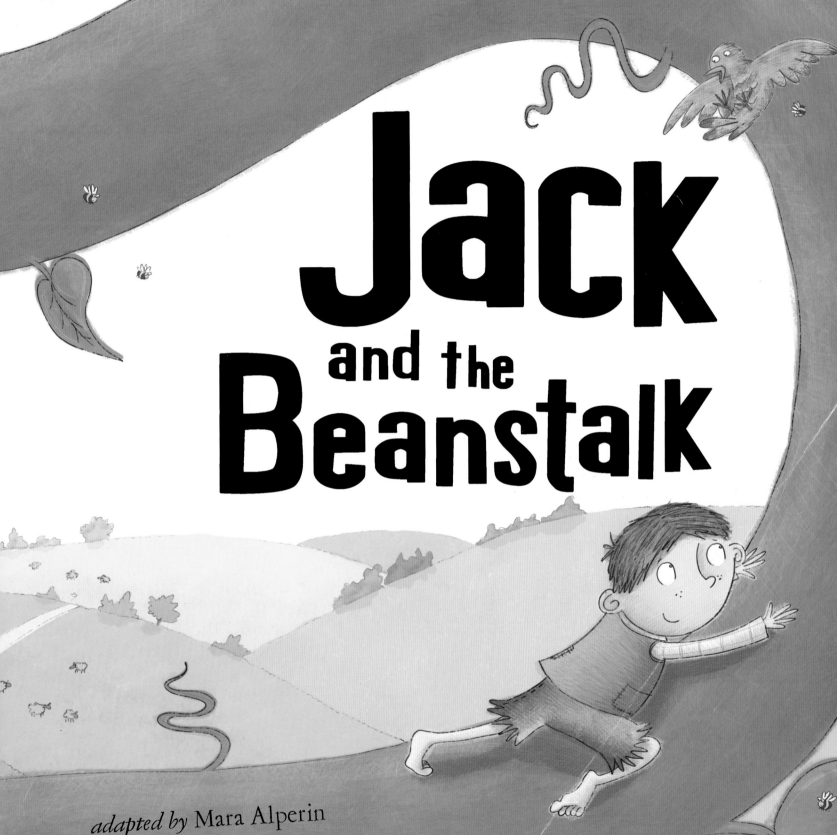

Jack
and the
Beanstalk

adapted by Mara Alperin

Illustrated by Mark Chambers

tiger tales

Deep in the countryside lived
a widow and her son, Jack.
Their cottage was crumbling,
and their clothes were patched.
They were very, very poor.

One day, Jack's mother said, "We must
sell our cow. Take her to market, Jack,
and bring home some gold pieces."
And so he set off to town.

But before Jack had gotten very far, he met
a strange little man.

"That's a fine cow," the man said.
"I'll swap you five **magic beans** for her."

"Magic beans?" said Jack. "Are they
really magic?"

"Magic they are, or chop off my beard and knit it into a sweater," croaked the little man.

Magic beans!

Jack couldn't wait to tell his mother. He clutched them tightly, and ran all the way home.

Jack's mother was **furious.**
"We need money, not useless old beans!"
she cried. And she threw them out
of the window in disgust.

But late that night,
a tiny bean sprout
poked out from the
ground.

And then it grew...

and grew...

and GREW!

The next morning, the beanstalk
stretched high into the sky.
"The beans *were* magic!" Jack cried.
"But what's at the top?"

Jack climbed up, up, up the

beanstalk.

At last, he reached the very top.
There, shimmering in the
sunlight, was . . .

...a magnificent castle!

Just then, Jack's stomach rumbled.
I must find some breakfast, he thought,
and he tapped on the castle door.

The door creaked open, and a huge giantess smiled down.

"Hello!" Jack shouted up. "Please, do you have any food?"

"YOU POOR THING!" boomed the giantess. "COME RIGHT IN! BUT QUICKLY, BEFORE THE GIANT GETS UP!"

What a marvelous feast! There was an **enormous** loaf of bread and a **gigantic** jar of jelly. Jack dug in at once.

But suddenly, the room
began to shake.

BOoM!
BOoM!
BOoM!

"OH MY GOODNESS!"
cried the giantess.
"HE'S COMING!"
And she shoved Jack under
a teacup to hide.

Into the room stomped a
big, scary, HUNGRY giant!

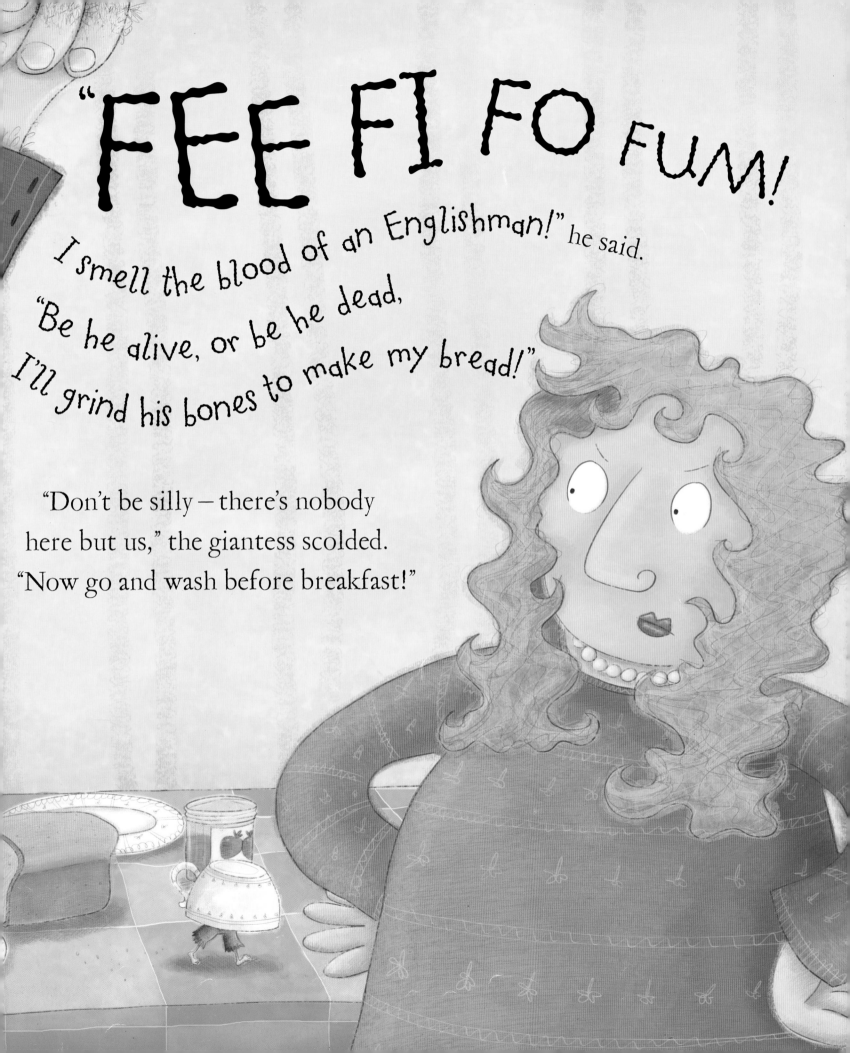

"FEE FI FO FUM!

I smell the blood of an Englishman!" he said.
"Be he alive, or be he dead,
I'll grind his bones to make my bread!"

"Don't be silly — there's nobody here but us," the giantess scolded. "Now go and wash before breakfast!"

Jack trembled. *I must leave—now!* he thought.

He was half way down the hall when he heard a . . .

"SQUAWK!"

It was a hen with bright golden feathers!

"Help!" she clucked. "Set me free and I'll lay you golden eggs every morning!"

Jack scooped up the hen, but then he heard huge footsteps **THUNDERING** after them . . . .

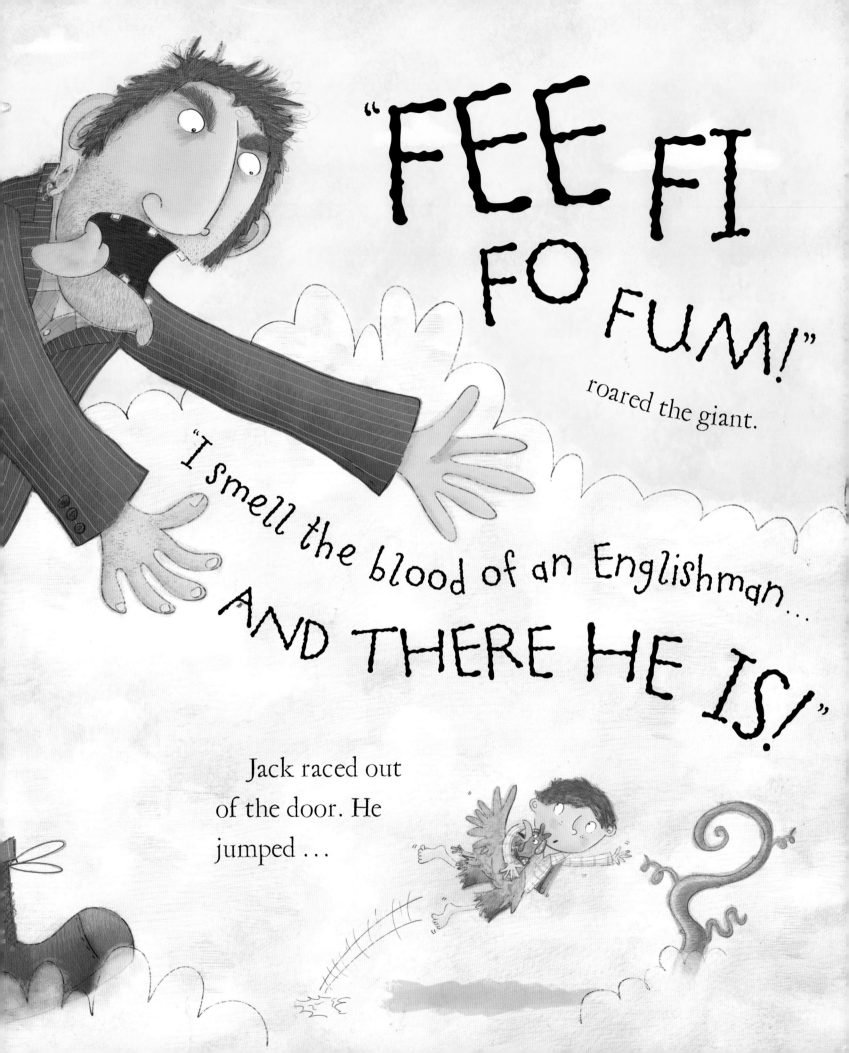

"FEE FI FO FUM!"

roared the giant.

"I smell the blood of an Englishman...
AND THERE HE IS!"

Jack raced out of the door. He jumped ...

... and slid
down the
beanstalk ...

down ...

down ...

down...

...all
the
way
back
to his
cottage.

"Mother!
Quick! Bring the
ax!" he shouted.

Jack's mother swung the ax at the beanstalk. **THWACK!**

It shuddered and shook, and then the giant came tumbling down!

"FEEEEEEE

FI FO . . . "

CRASH!

And that was the end of the giant.

Jack hugged his mother tight. "Look what I found!" he said, and he showed her the golden hen.

"Oh, Jack," said his mother. "I'm so glad you're safe. And you were right about those magic beans!"

So Jack, his mother, and the golden hen
all lived happily ever after. And with
lots of **golden eggs**, they were
never poor again!

Mara Alperin

Mara has adapted all of the books
in the My First Fairy Tales series, which includes
Little Red Riding Hood, *Goldilocks and the Three Bears*,
Jack and the Beanstalk, and *The Three Billy Goats Gruff*.
As a child, she loved listening to fairy tales and then retelling the stories
to her family and friends. Mara lives in London, England. When not
writing, she enjoys reading, baking, hiking, and
playing Ultimate Frisbee.

Mark Chambers

Mark is an award-winning illustrator of many picture books.
His previous books with Little Tiger Press include *Pigeon Poo*,
which won the Sheffield Picture Book Award in 2013. Another one
of his books, *Noisy Bottom*s, by Sam Taplin, was shortlisted for
the Roald Dahl Funny Prize 2013. Mark was the illustrator for
London Zoo's Animal Adventure children's zoo and also was chosen
for the Bear with Me collaborative project. He works in his studio,
which is a short walk from his house, and shares it with a lobster
called Larry, a monkey, and a pig named Pudding!